HOW TO DRAW™ OPTICAL ILLUSIONS

Mark Bergin

BOOK HOUSE

Published in Great Britain in MMXVI by
Book House, an imprint of
The Salariya Book Company Ltd
25 Marlborough Place, Brighton BN1 1UB
www.salariya.com

ISBN: 978-1-910706-57-2

3 5 7 9 8 6 4 2

A CIP catalogue record for this book is available from the British Library.

Printed and bound in China.

Reprinted in MMXVIII.

Author: Mark Bergin was born in Hastings in 1961. He studied at Eastbourne College of Art and has specialised in historical reconstructions as well as aviation and maritime subjects since 1983. He lives in Bexhill-on-Sea with his wife and three children.

Editor: Nick Pierce

Visit
www.salariya.com
for our online catalogue and
free fun stuff.

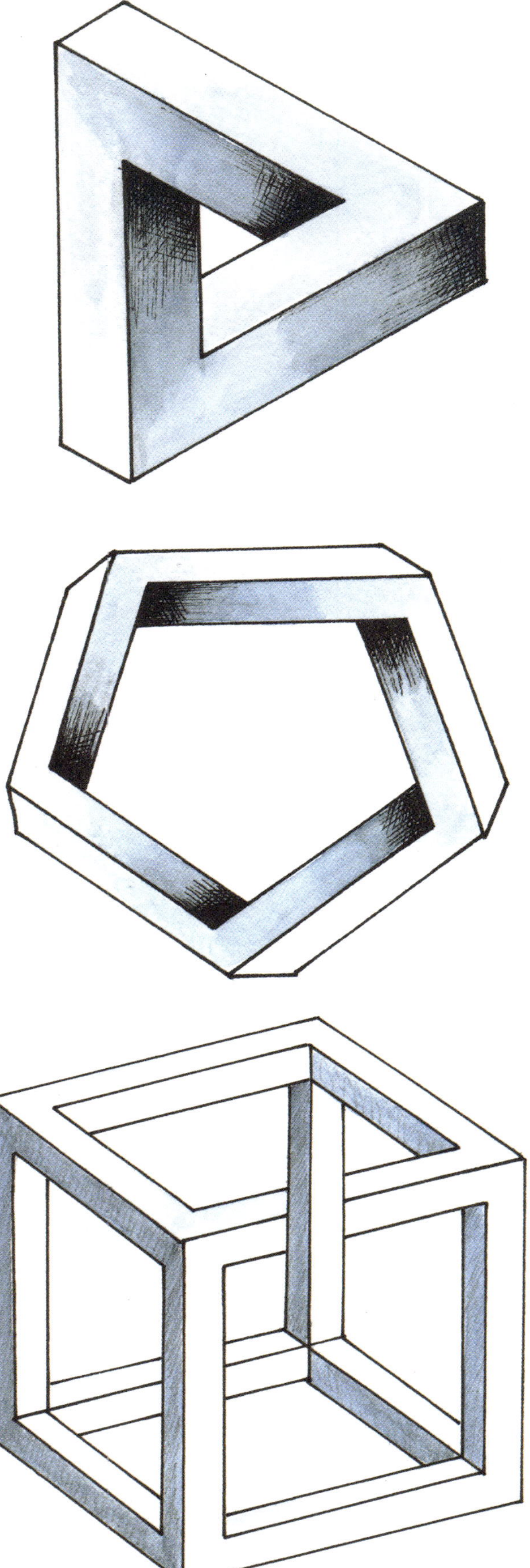

Contents

Introduction

An optical illusion is an image designed to trick the eye into perceiving it differently from how it actually looks. Amaze your friends by drawing some of the many different illusions shown on the following pages.

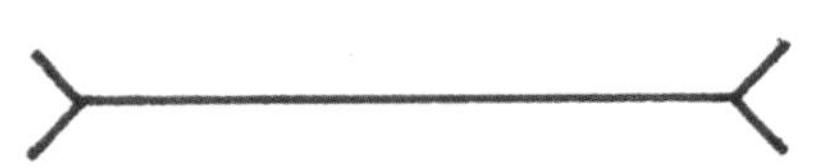

Changing the direction of the arrows makes the lower horizontal line look as if it is longer.

These two black dots are actually the same size although the one inside the small circle appears bigger.

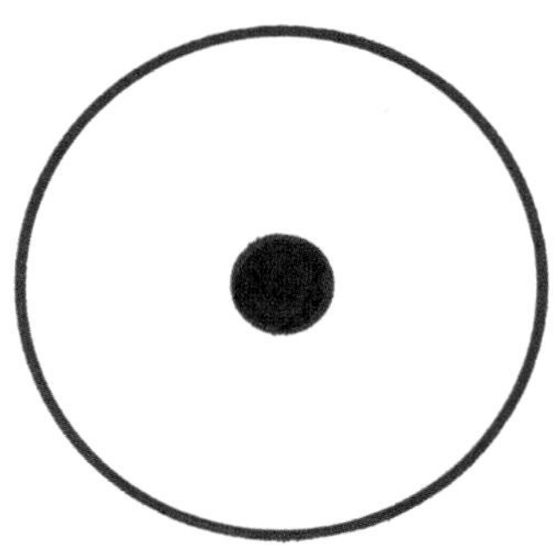

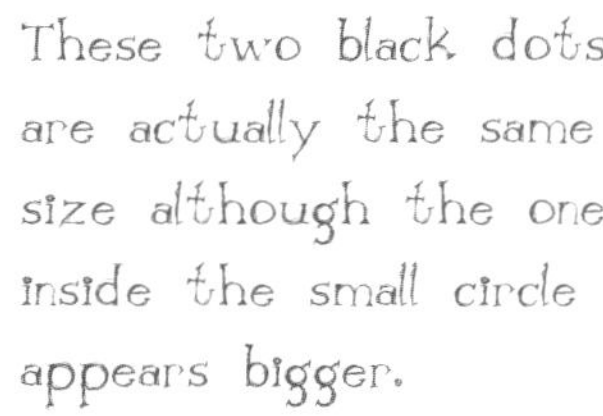

The use of differently-sized dots makes this picture look as if it is a series of curves.

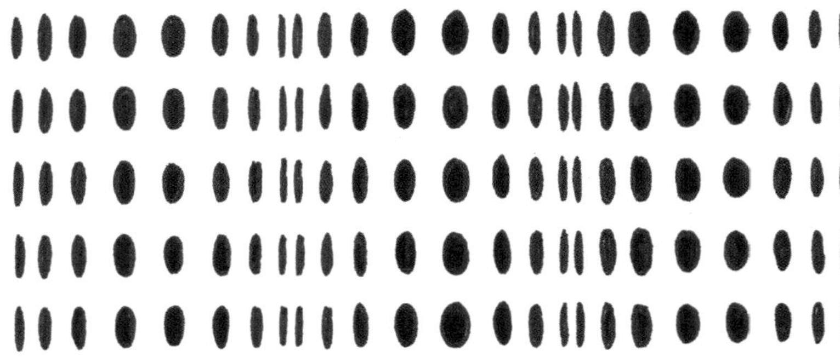

All of these vertical lines of squares are the same width even though it looks as if some are bulging.

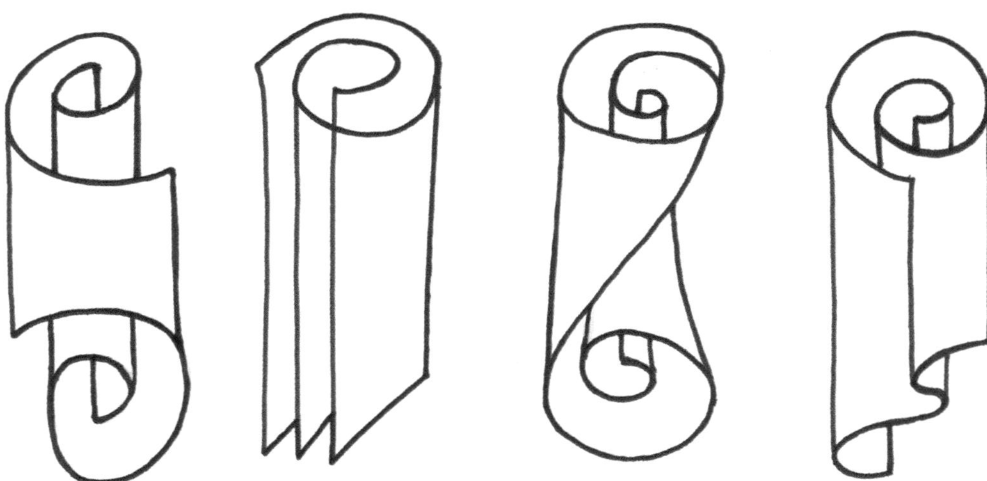

These scrolls are completely contradictory and can be created easily. Imagine two or more contrasting viewpoints of the rolled sheet and blend them together.

These are known as Necker's Cubes. The transparent cube frames offer no cues about their depth, so your brain keeps interpreting their shape differently.

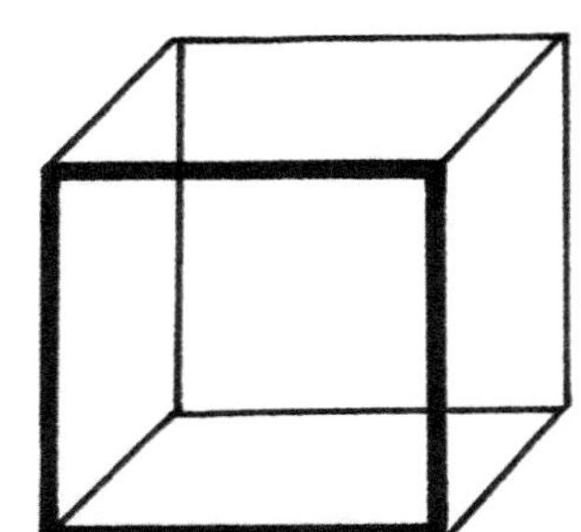

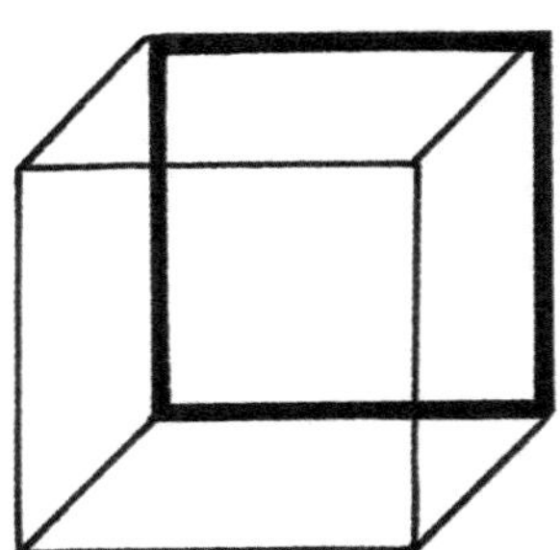

This picture is composed of four black arrows. Can you also see the four hidden arrows pointing towards the centre?

These simple patterns create shapes which appear to be both concave and converse at the same time.

Face or vase?

This optical illusion uses negative space to create two distinct images out of one simple drawing. The image can be seen as silhouetted portraits or a vase.

Start by drawing a face in profile.

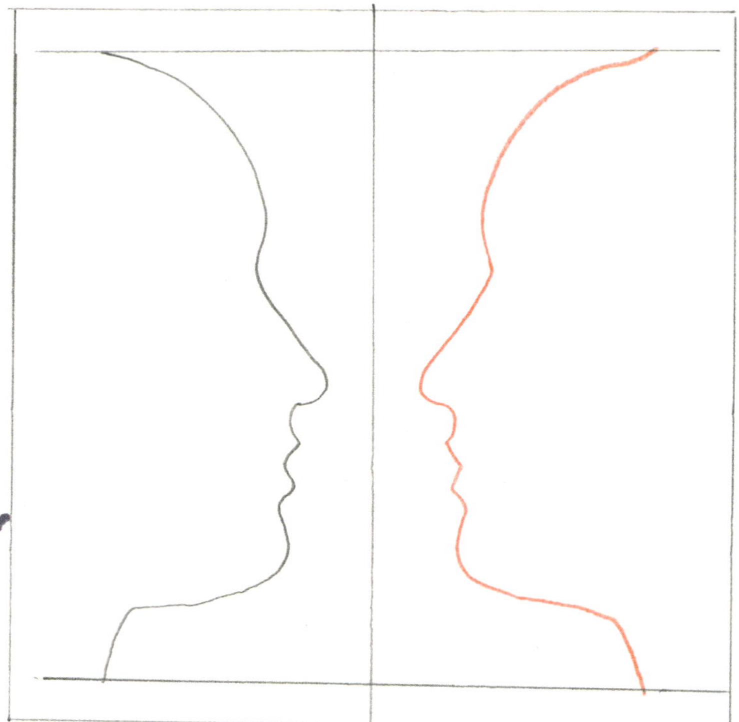

Now reverse and draw the outline of the face. This creates the shape of a vase, too.

Shading in the faces emphasises the duality of the image.

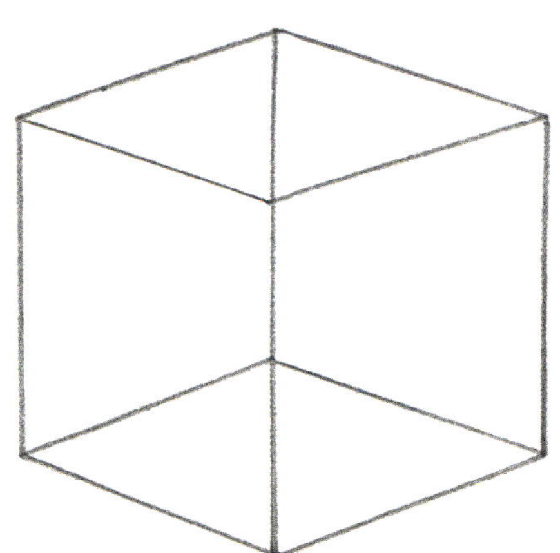

Start by drawing a transparent cube like the one shown here.

Now begin attaching additional identical cubes to the original, building up a pattern of boxes as illustrated.

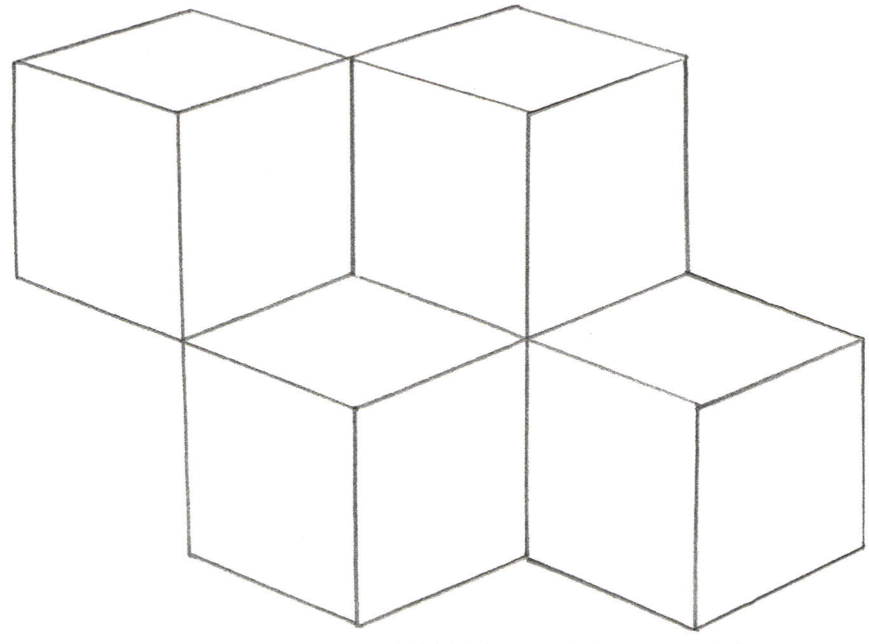

Shade in the faces of the cubes to make them look more solid and three-dimensional.

Depending on how you look at the picture, it can seem as if the cubes are visible from above or visible from below.

Spiral square

This design uses a simple geometric formula to create the illusion of movement and depth. The whirling, spiral effect is the result of stepped directional changes, combined with ever diminishing scale.

Start by drawing a large square.

Now draw a second square, turned 5 degrees around the centre of the first. This square will become slightly reduced to fit within the area.

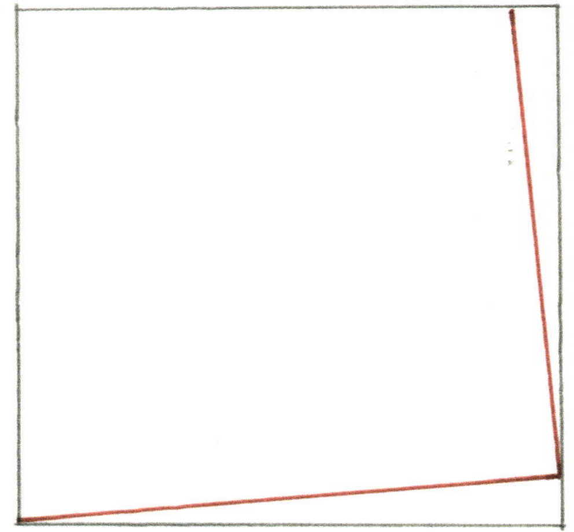

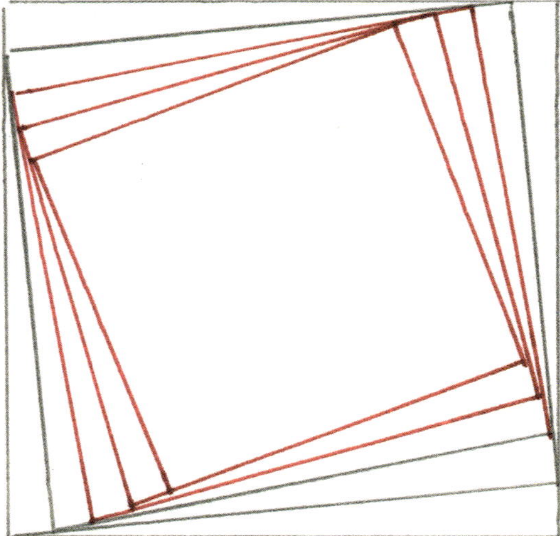

Repeat. Every subsequent square will gradually decrease in size. The corners of each should touch the sides of the previous square.

Now use a black felt tip pen to block in alternate areas (as shown). This bold black and white pattern gives the image a more hypnotic and striking visual impact.

Erase any unwanted pencil lines.

Optical stripes

Optical stripes can create weird and wonderful distorted 3D effects on a flat sheet of paper.

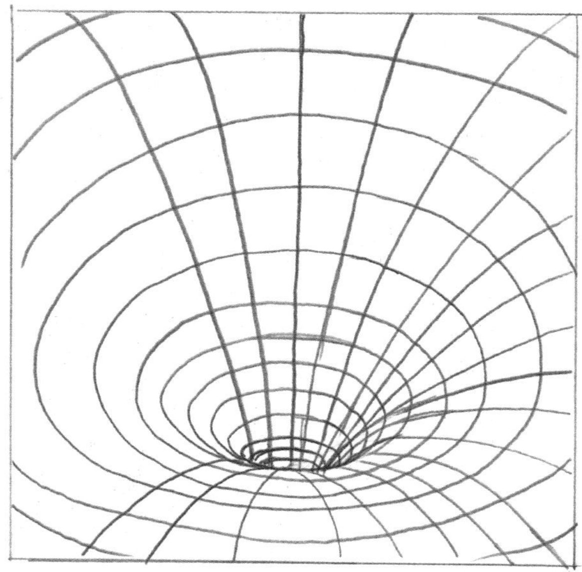

1. Draw a wavy line on a piece of medium weight card.

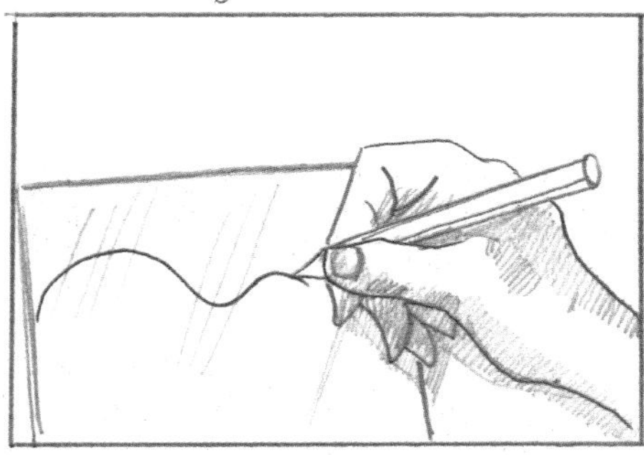

2. Cut along the line as accurately as possible.

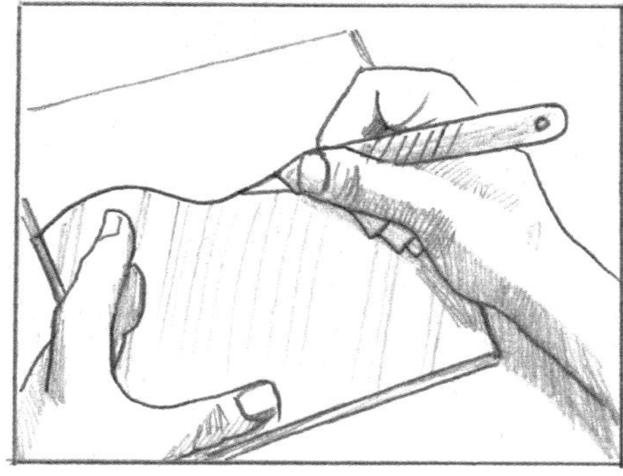

3. Use as a template to draw wavy lines covering one sheet of paper..

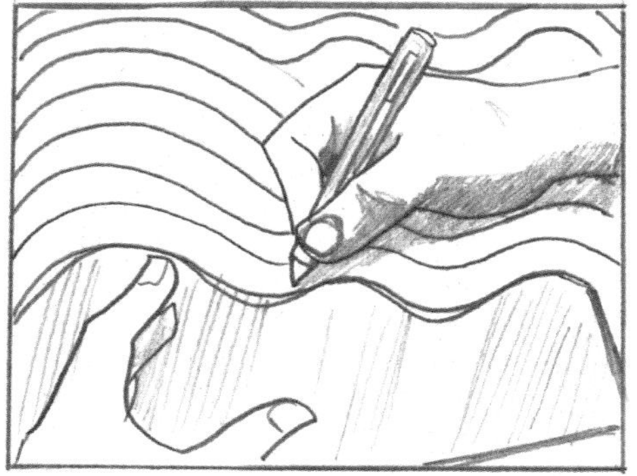

4. Carefully shade in each alternate stripe in black or a bold colour.

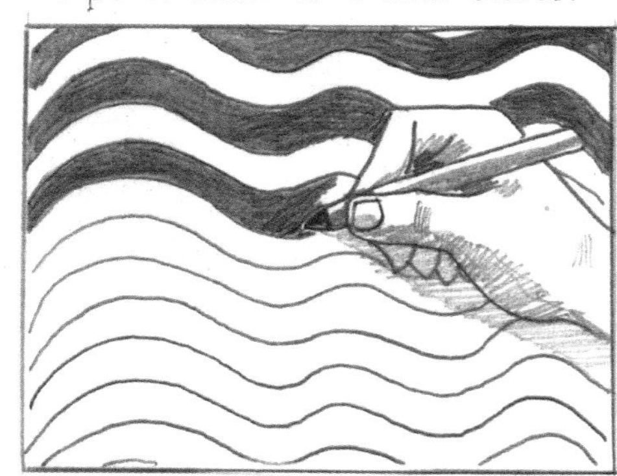

The template was gradually moved downwards in a diagonal direction to get this effect of cascading lines.

These are similar curves reversed and spaced at regular intervals horizontally.

Erase any unwanted pencil lines.

Impossible shapes

Impossible objects are disturbing because the brain always unconsciously seeks to interpret two-dimensional drawings as three-dimensional shapes. When the brain is presented with a drawn shape that could not possibly exist it is thrown into confusion as to how to interpret the visual data.

This impossible shape is called the Penrose Tribar.

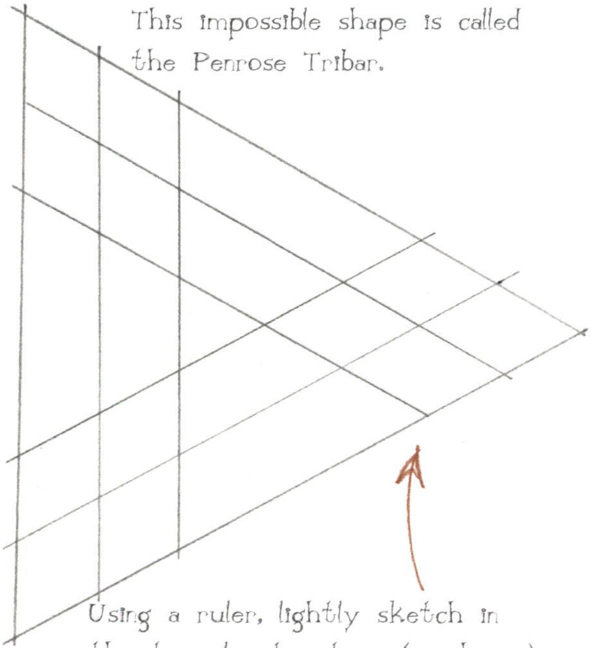

Using a ruler, lightly sketch in the triangle structure (as shown).

Draw a short line across each corner.

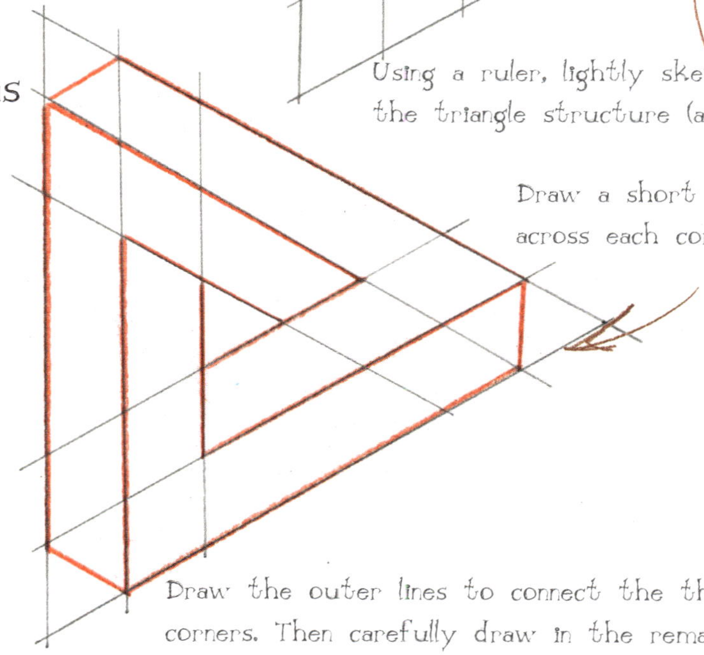

Draw the outer lines to connect the three corners. Then carefully draw in the remaining lines (as shown).

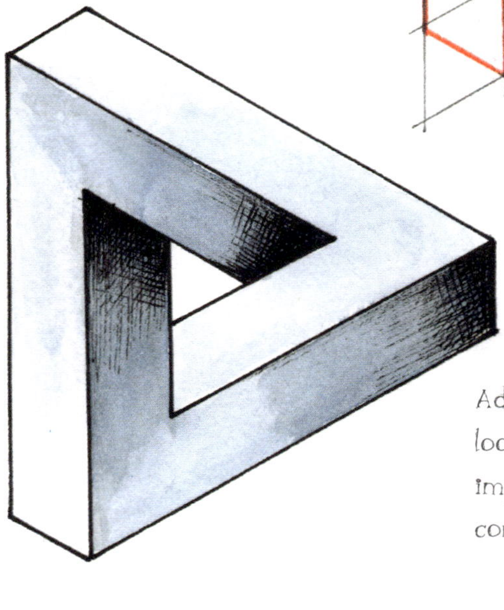

Add shading and colour to make the image look more realistic. This will make the impossibility of the shape all the more confusing.

Your impossible shapes could have any number of sides, planes, colours and textures.

The only limit to designing impossible shapes is your own imagination.

Erase any unwanted pencil lines.

Impossible shapes continued

These prong and fork images are impossible objects that confuse the eye and brain by combining conflicting messages. The usual cues for depth or position do not correspond as expected, which creates a bizarre optical effect.

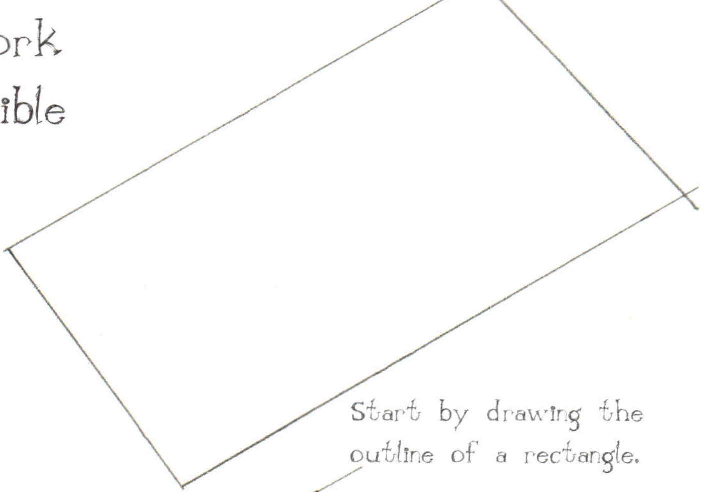

Start by drawing the outline of a rectangle.

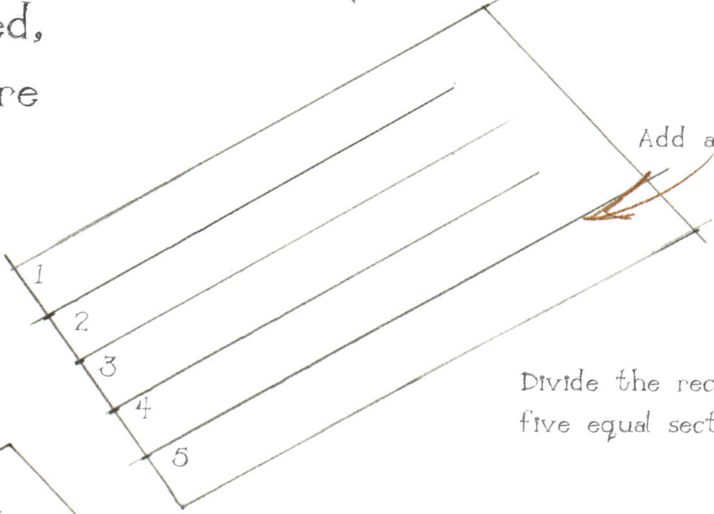

Add another line.

1
2
3
4
5

Divide the rectangle into five equal sections.

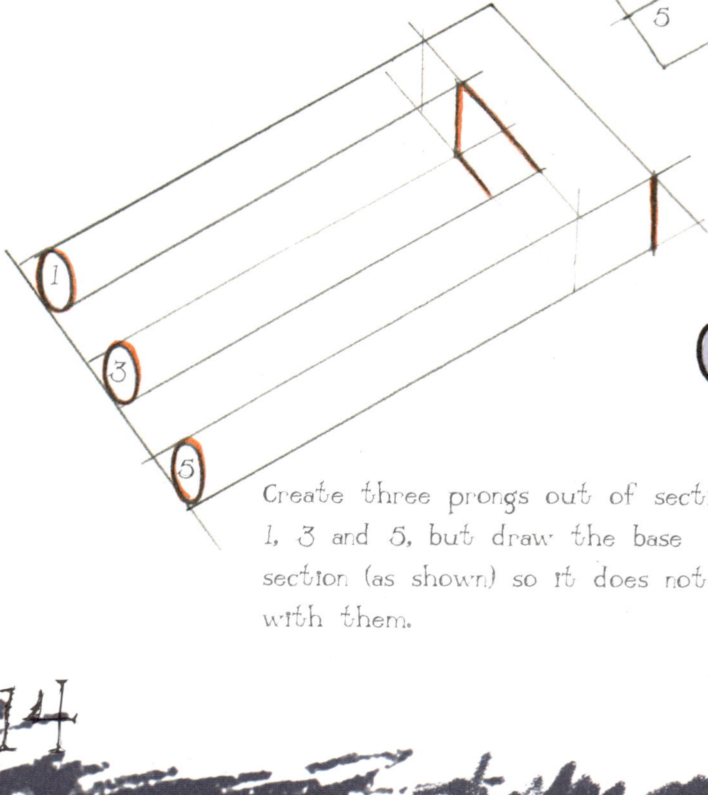

1
3
5

Create three prongs out of sections 1, 3 and 5, but draw the base section (as shown) so it does not align with them.

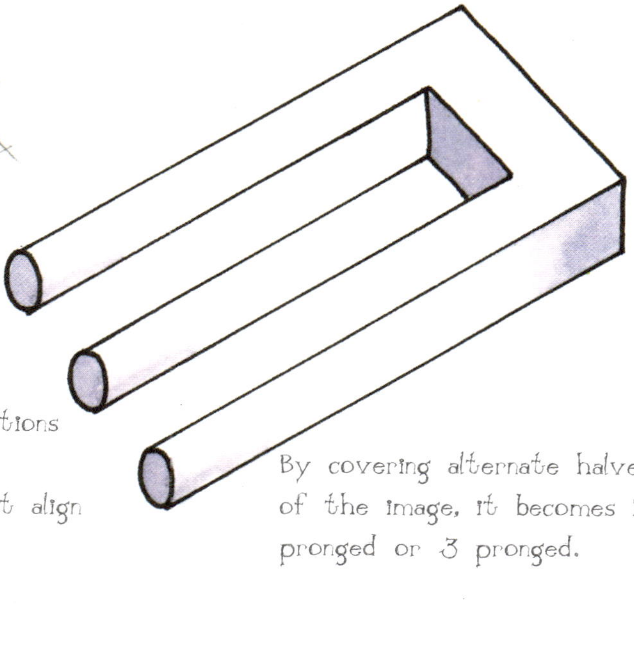

By covering alternate halves of the image, it becomes 2 pronged or 3 pronged.

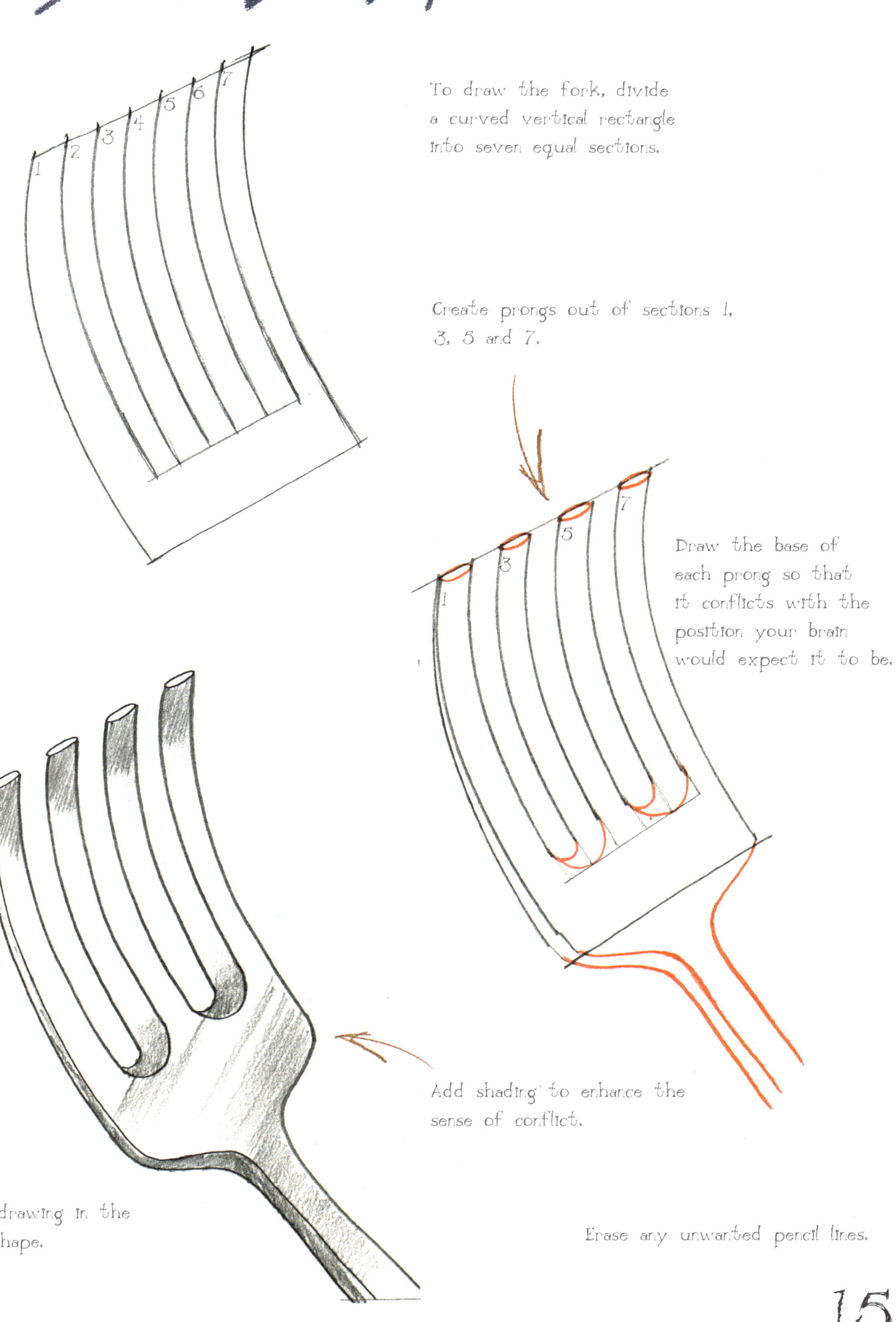

To draw the fork, divide a curved vertical rectangle into seven equal sections.

Create prongs out of sections 1, 3, 5 and 7.

Draw the base of each prong so that it conflicts with the position your brain would expect it to be.

Add shading to enhance the sense of conflict.

Finish drawing in the fork shape.

Erase any unwanted pencil lines.

Impossible ring and box

Weirdly, it is possible to represent impossible figures as if they are physical models that could exist in three-dimensional space. If depicted and viewed from a specific angle, our brain can misinterpret such shapes as solid sculptures.

Start by drawing two concentric circles, one large and one smaller.

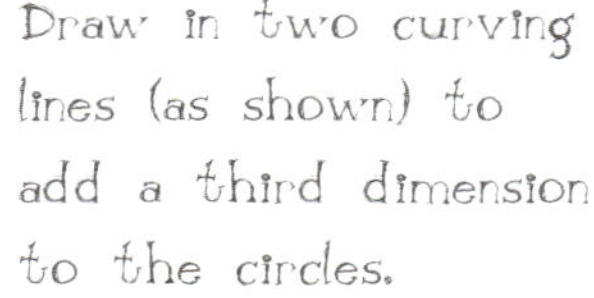

Draw in two curving lines (as shown) to add a third dimension to the circles.

Add colour to the image to give it more solidity. Experiment by trying to depict it from different angles.

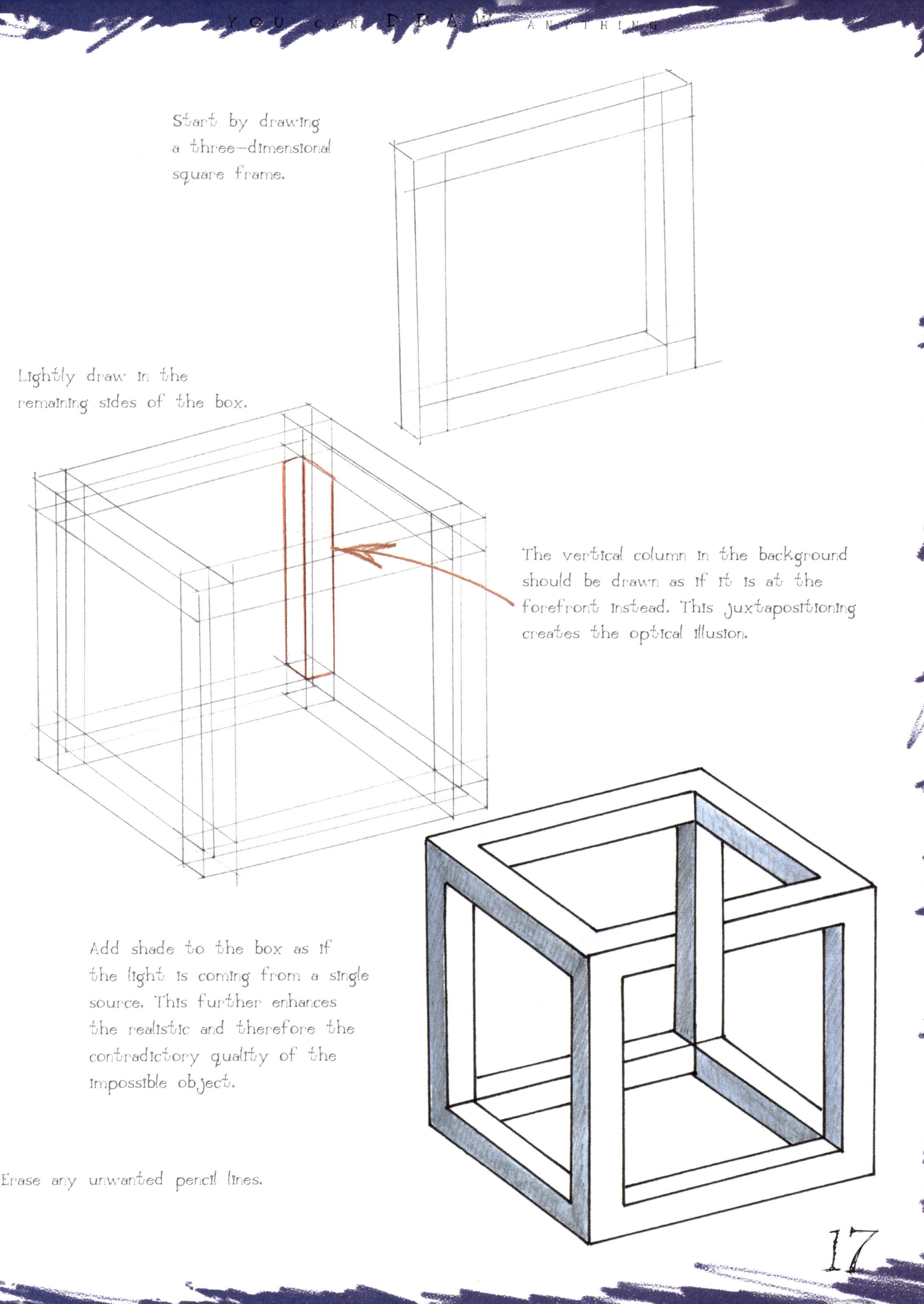

Start by drawing a three-dimensional square frame.

Lightly draw in the remaining sides of the box.

The vertical column in the background should be drawn as if it is at the forefront instead. This juxtapositioning creates the optical illusion.

Add shade to the box as if the light is coming from a single source. This further enhances the realistic and therefore the contradictory quality of the impossible object.

Erase any unwanted pencil lines.

Seeing is believing... or is it?

In each picture, all the figures are the same height, but appear smaller or larger. This is due to the effect of placing the figures within the converging lines of perspective which confuses the eye.

Confusing the eye

In a normal drawing, the relationship between an object and its surroundings – known as the 'figure-ground' – is stable. However, it is possible to create optical illusions where that relationship is ambiguous and figures can be hidden in the background or become the background itself.

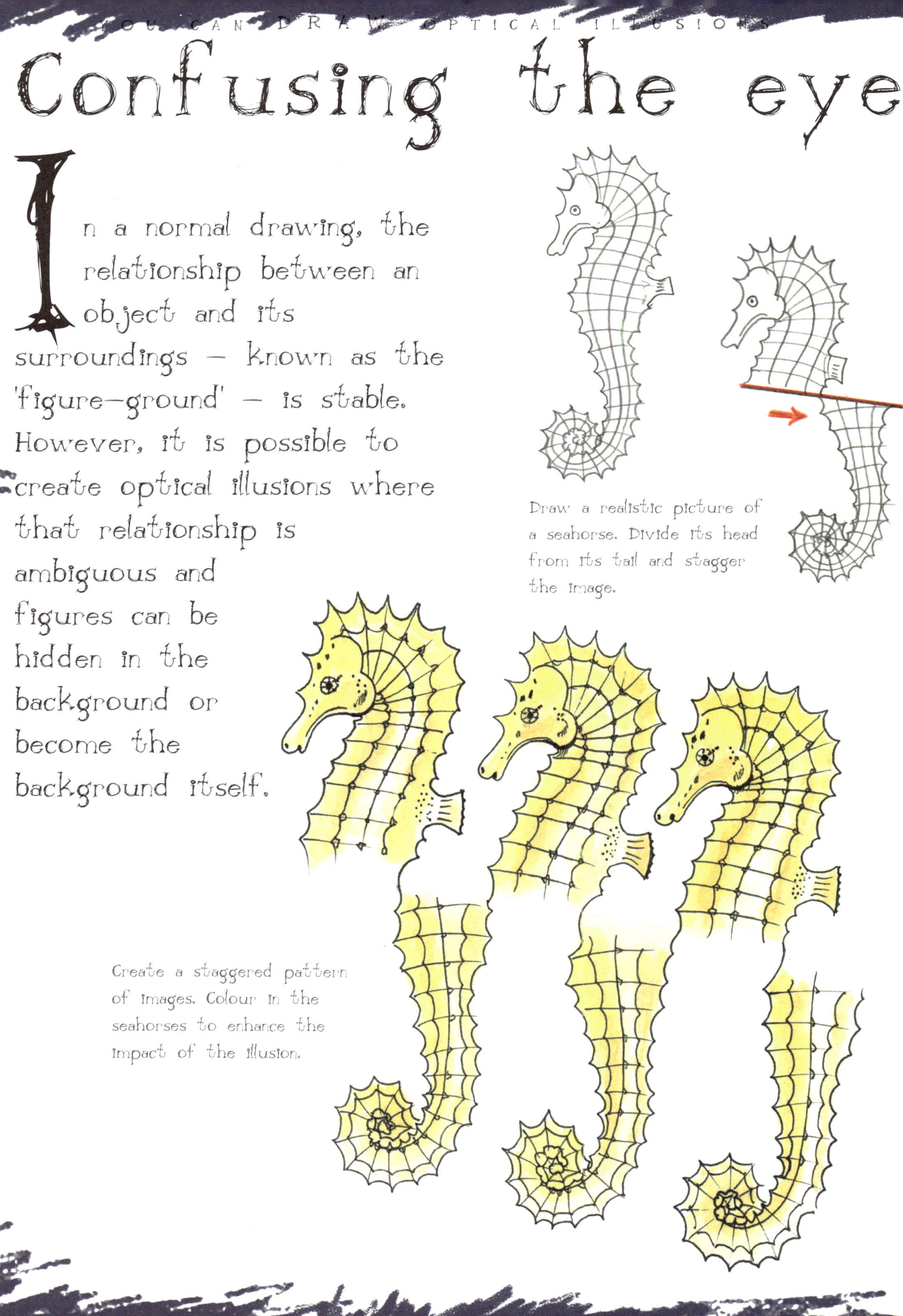

Draw a realistic picture of a seahorse. Divide its head from its tail and stagger the image.

Create a staggered pattern of images. Colour in the seahorses to enhance the impact of the illusion.

1. Lightly pencil in an elephant.

2. This trick relies on optically moving the legs (1–3) forward. Erase the first foot and transpose it onto the empty space in front of the leg. Do the same with the second and third legs. This creates space to add an extra rear leg. Now you have a five-legged elephant!

3. Add shading and texture. These realistic touches will further confuse the perceptions of this surreal image.

Erase any unwanted pencil lines.

Never-ending staircase

The Penrose Stairs is an impossible object invented by the mathematicians Lionel and Roger Penrose. It was made famous by the graphic artist M. C. Escher, who depicted the staircase in an image known as 'Ascending and Descending'.

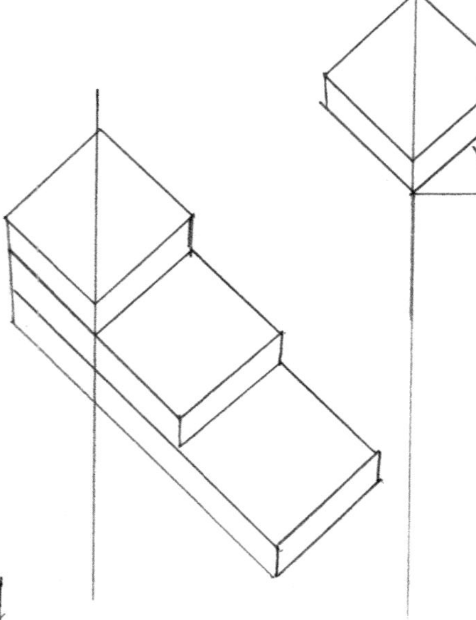

Draw four connecting staircases at 90 degree angles to each other.

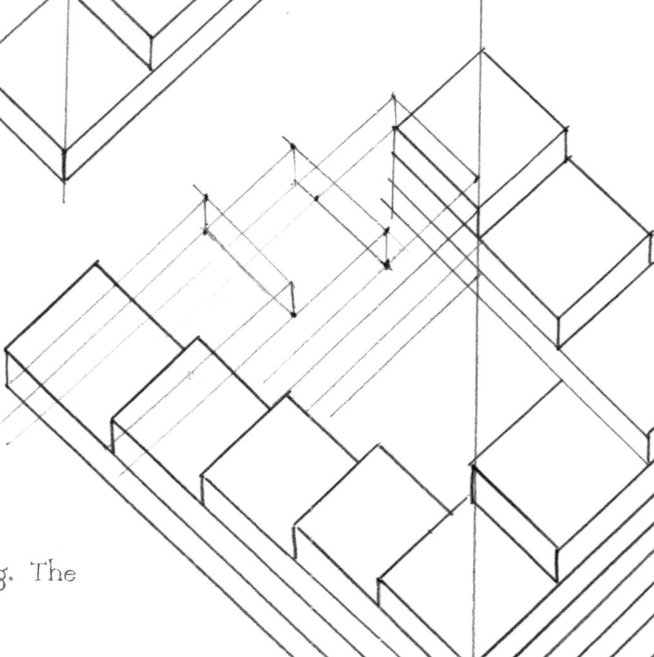

The righthand staircases should be ascending. The lefthand staircases should be descending.

The complete staircase will now look as if it forms a continuous loop.

Draw in figures ascending the stairs. Add shadows from conflicting light sources to add a final surreal touch to this confusing image.

Erase any unwanted pencil lines.

Topsy turvy heads

Topsy turvy heads play on the perceptions of the human brain. Even though the facial features have been jumbled up in a manner that is nonsensical, your brain still recognises the image as a human face.

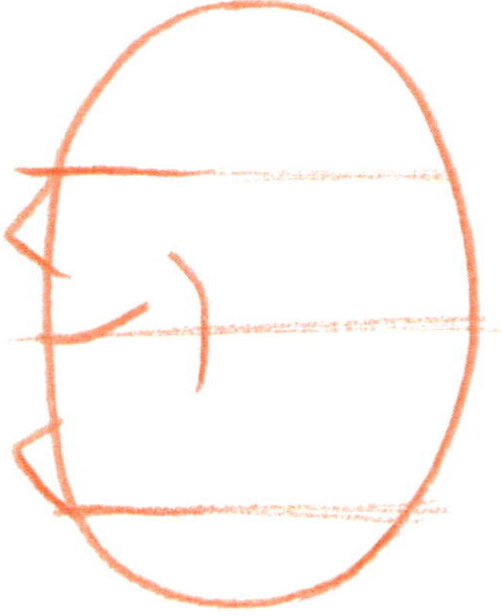

First, draw an oval for the head. Add lines to position the basic facial features.

Add more detail: the eyes, the outline of the headscarf and the collar.

Complete the knotted headscarf and draw in the rest of the collar. Add texture and patterns to bring the image to life. Now look at your drawing in reverse!

Draw an oval. Sketch in a vertical and horizontal line through the centre to position the eyes and the ears.

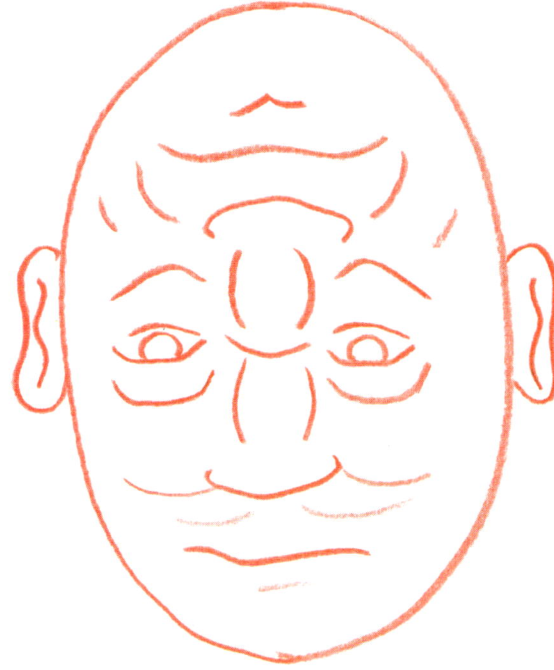

Add further details: mouth, bags under the eyes, eyebrows, wrinkles and frown lines.

Add pupils to the eyes. Draw in a beard and hat (as shown) or a head of hair. Add shading and texture. Now look at your drawing in reverse!

Erase any unwanted pencil lines.

Hidden pictures

It's possible to create pictures containing hidden images or details that only eagle-eyed viewers will spot.

Draw in the outline of the child. Now sketch in all the hidden faces in the surroundings.

Add more detail to the background. Use shading and texture to cleverly conceal the faces so that they are not instantly visible and must be 'discovered'.

Create a finished drawing of a boy's face to use as your template. Trace the outline and facial features, then sketch in trees and branches that depict the same contours. The face should be apparent, yet elusive.

Add more trees, leaves and birds as required to complete the image. Do not overwork it so the boy's face remains quite subtle.

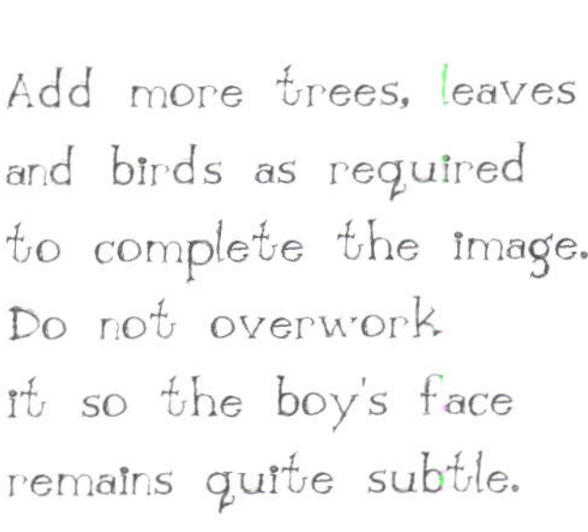

Erase any unwanted pencil lines.

Ribbon head

A spiralling ribbon formation creates the fragmented three-dimensional portrait of a woman. The ribbon head is another optical illusion popularised by M.C. Escher.

Start by drawing a straightforward portrait image.

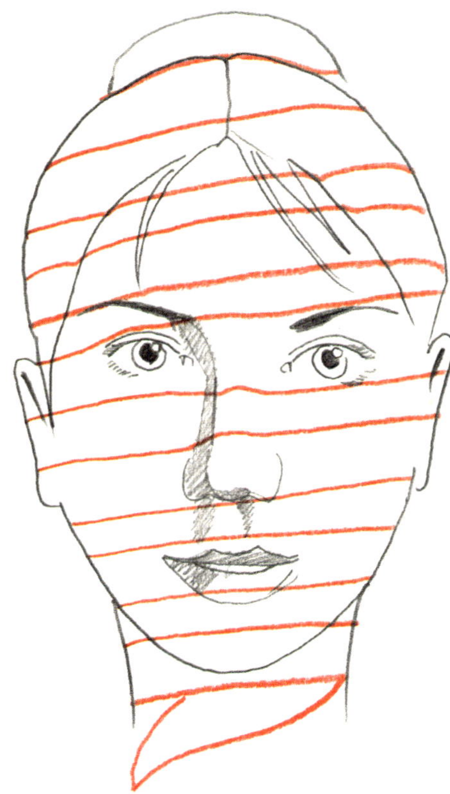

Superimpose the shape of a tapering ribbon over the top of the face. The ribbon shape must cover the eyes, nose and mouth. Erase any part of the face that lies outside the ribbon contour.

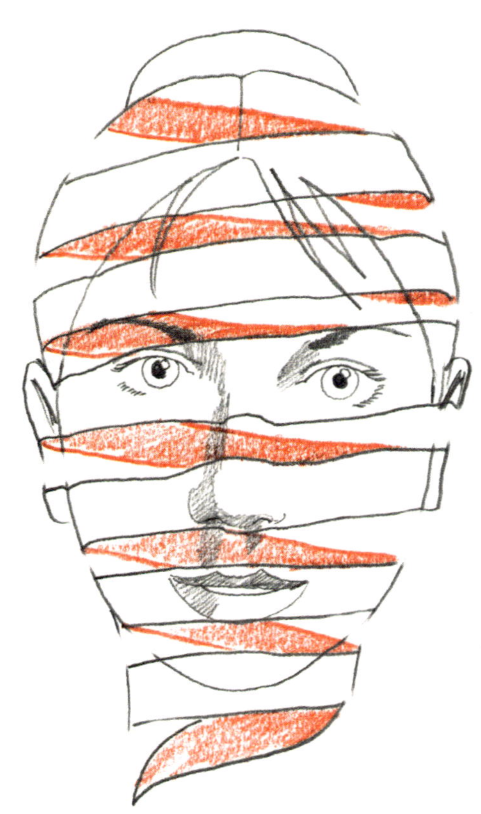

Complete the details of the face and add shading to make it more realistic.

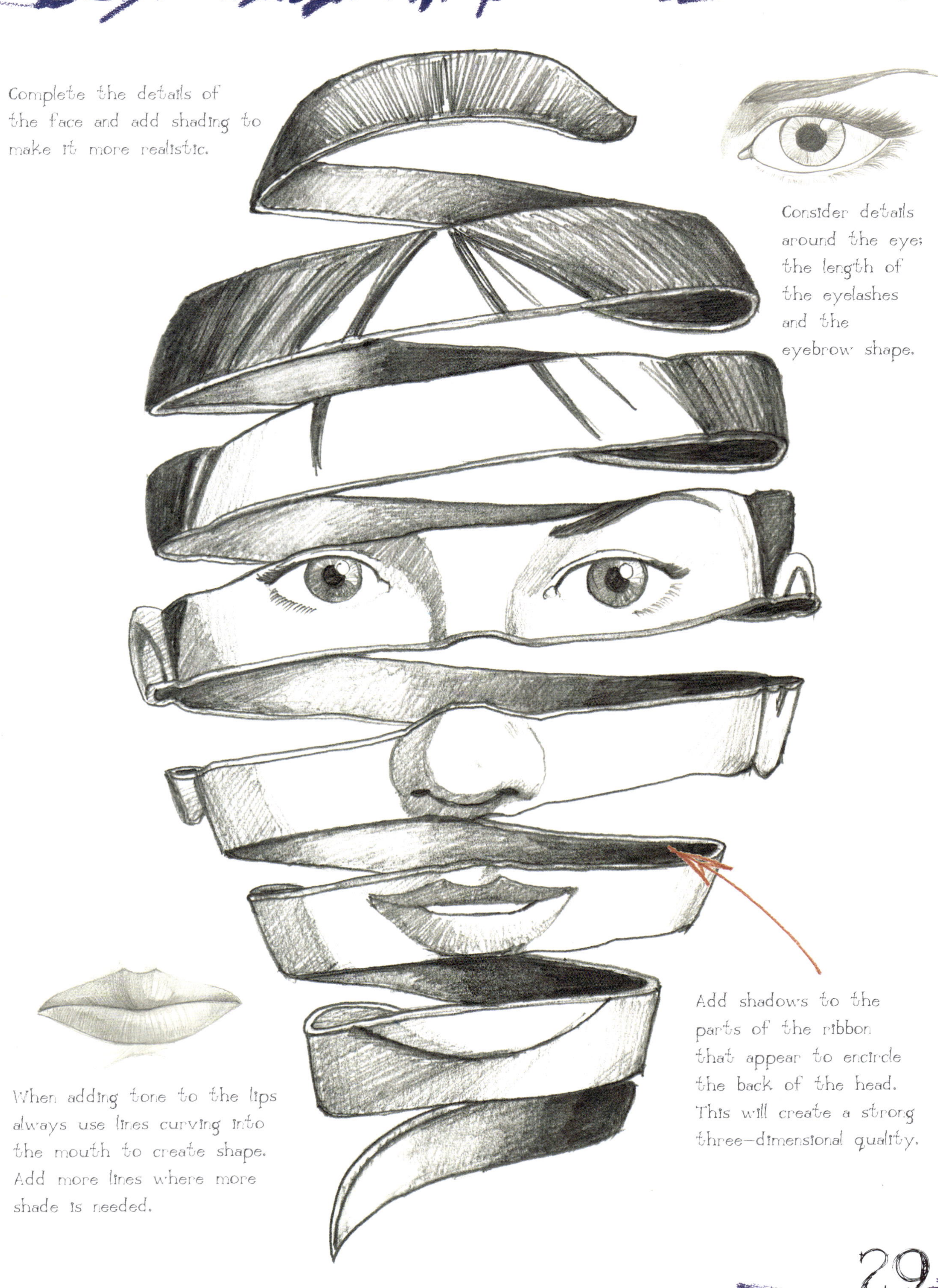

Consider details around the eye; the length of the eyelashes and the eyebrow shape.

Add shadows to the parts of the ribbon that appear to encircle the back of the head. This will create a strong three-dimensional quality.

When adding tone to the lips always use lines curving into the mouth to create shape. Add more lines where more shade is needed.

Secret skull

Skulls form a visually striking element that is conducive to all manner of surreal imagery. This universally recognised and powerful symbol can be used to great effect to create a more eye-catching image.

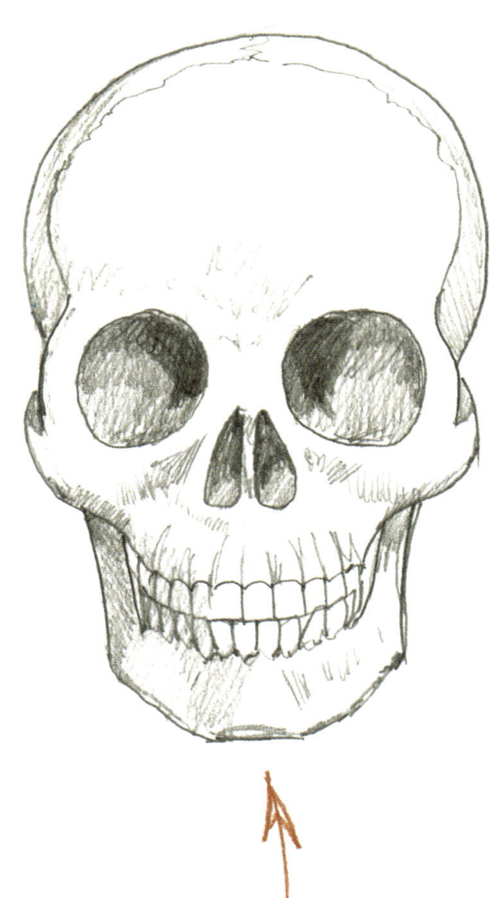

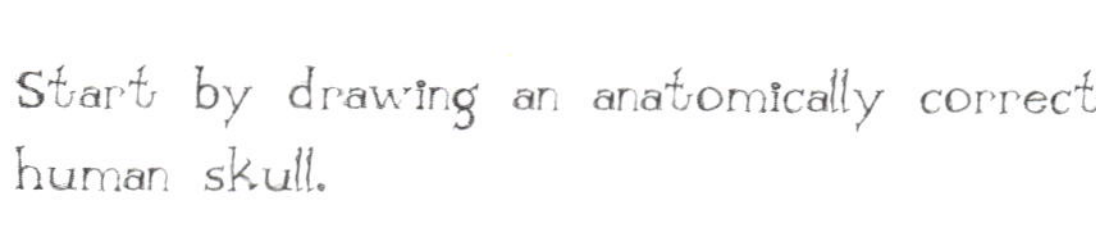

Start by drawing an anatomically correct human skull.

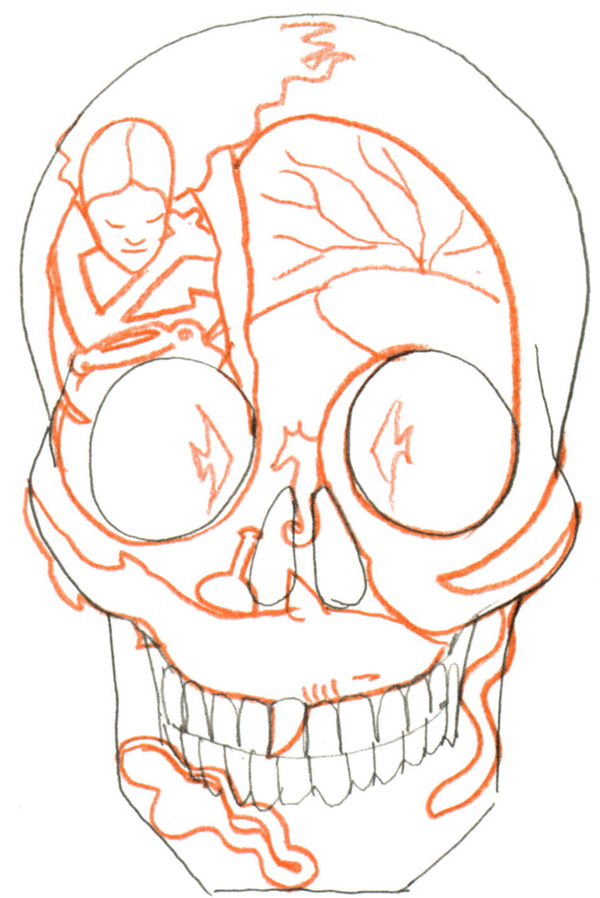

Now start to overlay parts of the skull with objects and creatures that portray the underwater theme of the drawing.

Carefully shade in the eye sockets of the skull. This creates a dramatic illusion of three-dimensional depth.

Add additional details to the drawing, such as the scales and jewellery worn by the mermaid or the patterns on the sea creatures. Surround the skull with a tangle of seaweed and coral to create added interest.

Glossary

Concave A surface or outline that curves inwards.

Construction lines Guidelines used in the early stages of a drawing; they may be erased later.

Converse A surface or outline that curves outwards.

Geometric shape A shape made of regular lines or sides.

Light source The direction from which the light seems to come in a drawing.

Negative space The space between and surrounding the figures and objects depicted in an image.

Optical Relating to sight and visual information.

Perspective Representing two-dimensional objects in such a way that they appear to have the same qualities of depth and position in relation to each other as they would do in the three-dimensional world.

Index